DISCARD

Share, Big BEAR, SHARE!

by **Maureen Wright**

illustrated by
Will Hillenbrand

two lions

Published by Two Lions, New York
www.apub.com

Amazon, the Amazon logo, and Two Lions are trademarks
of Amazon.com, Inc., or its affiliates.

ISBN-13: 9781503951006 (hardcover)
ISBN-10: 1503951006 (hardcover)

The artwork for this book was created with graphite pencil and digital media.
Printed in China
First edition

1 3 5 7 9 10 8 6 4 2

Dedicated with much love to my grandsons,
Caleb and Samuel Wright
—M.W.

To Ruri, who knows how to share
—W.H.

Big Bear smiled and rubbed his tummy.
The berries he'd picked were very yummy!
He lounged by a tree and laughed with glee.
"These berries," he said, "are just for me!"

Birds and squirrels and two little mice
thought the berries looked very nice!

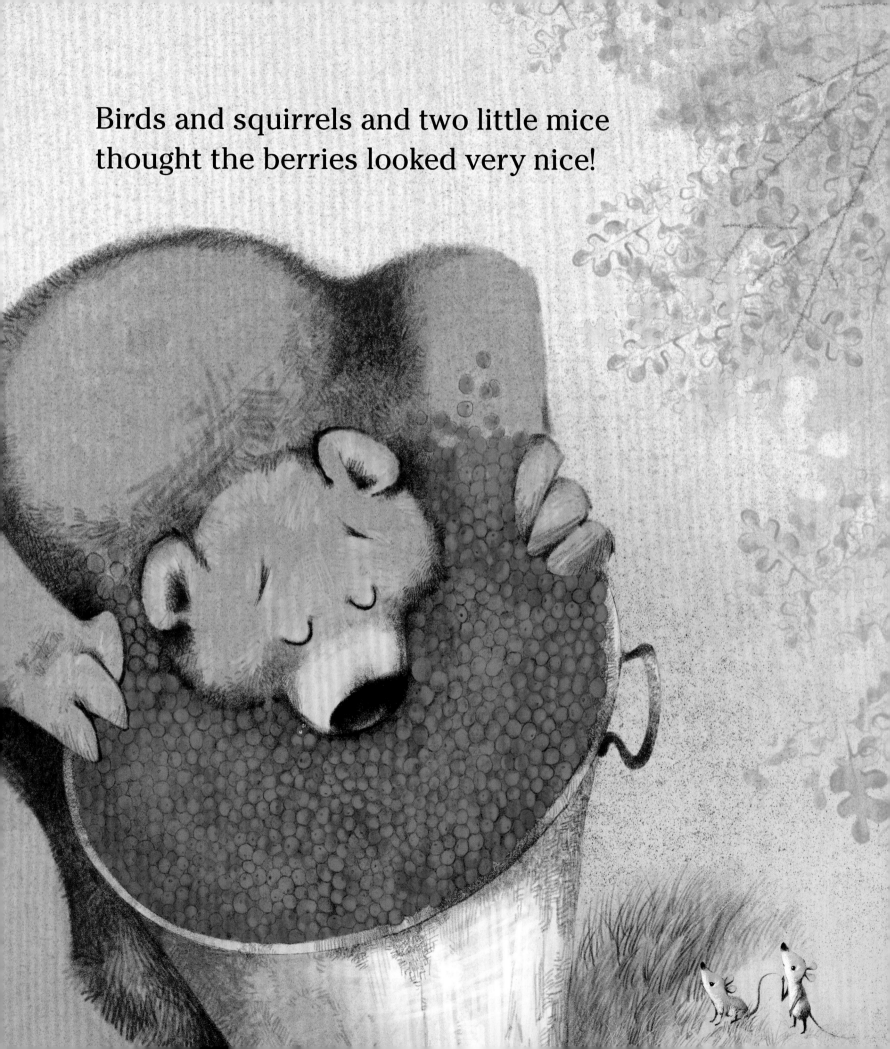

But Bear just sighed with a dreamy grin,
hugged his pail, and dug right in!

Branches shook on the old oak tree.
A deep, low voice said, "Listen to me. . . .

"Share, Big Bear, share!"

Somehow Bear misunderstood.
He didn't pay attention like a good bear should.

He thought Tree said
in the deep green woods,
"Hair, Big Bear, hair!"

"My hair?" said Bear.
"Are you sure?
All right, I guess
I'll comb my fur."

He slicked his fur back nice and neat,
then picked a berry and started to eat.

His friend Little Rabbit and a curious deer
smelled the berries and tiptoed near.

Branches shook on the old oak tree.
A deep, low voice said, "Listen to me. . . .

"Share,
Big Bear,
share!"

Somehow Bear misunderstood.
He didn't pay attention like a good bear should.
He thought Tree said in the deep, green woods,
"Lair, Big Bear, lair."

"Lair means home," said Bear. "It's true.
So I'll go home like he told me to."

He lumbered nearby to his cozy den,
peeked in the window at home and then . . .

. . . scampered back to the old oak tree
and gobbled berries merrily.

Branches shook on the old oak tree.
A deep, low voice said,
"Listen to me. . . .

"Share,
Big Bear,
share!"

Somehow Bear misunderstood.
He didn't pay attention like a good bear should.
He thought Tree said in the deep, green woods,

"Chair, Big Bear, chair."

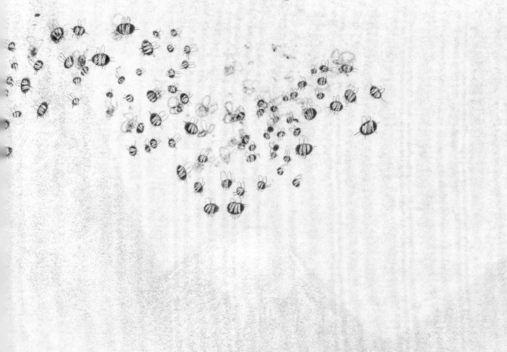

He found a stump and rolled it over,
swerving around the bee-filled clover.

He plopped his rump on the smooth tree stump and popped in a berry so juicy and plump.

Branches shook on the old oak tree.
A deep, low voice said, "Listen to me. . . .

"Share,
Big Bear,
share!"

Somehow Bear misunderstood.
He didn't pay attention like a good bear should.
He thought Tree said in the deep, green woods,
"Scare, Big Bear, scare!"

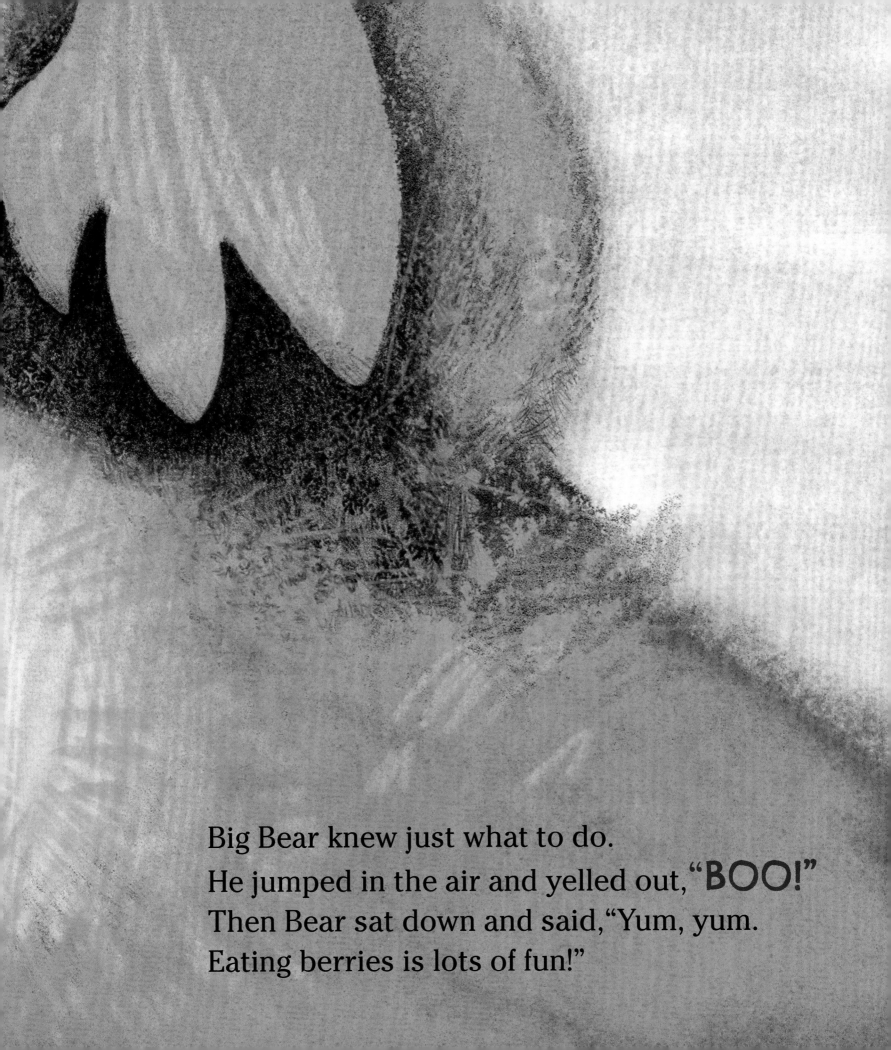

Big Bear knew just what to do.

He jumped in the air and yelled out, "BOO!"

Then Bear sat down and said, "Yum, yum.

Eating berries is lots of fun!"

The old tree yelled, "Be nice and share!
Don't you know that's only fair?
You like it when friends **share** with YOU!
It's the thoughtful thing to do!

"Share, Big Bear, share!"

"Well," said Bear,
"you could have told me before!"

He turned to his friends on the forest floor.
"Forgive me, please," he nicely said.
"I'm all mixed up inside my head!"

"How could I forget to share?
Come, everyone,
there are berries to spare!"

His friends said, "Thank you! These are sweet.
We're glad you shared your summertime treat."

"I like to share."

Big Bear sighed.

"It makes me happy deep inside."
They gobbled berries and giggled with glee
beneath the shade of the old oak tree!